DEADLY DISEASES

SMALLPOX

BY TAMMY GAGNE

CONTENT CONSULTANT
Sharon Medcalf, PhD
Assistant Professor, Department of Epidemiology
College of Public Health, University of Nebraska Medical Center

Core Library

An Imprint of Abdo Publishing
abdobooks.com

Cover image: Thanks to a successful vaccination campaign, the smallpox virus no longer circulates in the wild.

abdobooks.com

Published by Abdo Publishing, a division of ABDO, PO Box 398166, Minneapolis, Minnesota 55439.

Printed in the United States of America, North Mankato, Minnesota.
102021
012022

THIS BOOK CONTAINS RECYCLED MATERIALS

Cover Photo: Shutterstock Images
Interior Photos: Bettmann/Getty Images, 4–5; Dalmas/Sipa/AP Images, 7; Eye of Science/Science Source, 10, 45; Wellcome Collection/Science Source, 12–13; Red Line Editorial, 15, 37; National Library of Medicine/Science Source, 17; Everett Collection/Shutterstock Images, 19, 22, 43; Science Source, 21; 3D4Medical/Science Source, 24–25; Tim Vernon, LTH NHS Trust/Science Source, 26; Science Photo Library/Science Source, 30; Jean-Loup Charmet/Science Source, 32–33; New York Public Library/Science Source, 35; Los Angeles Examiner/University of Southern California/Corbis Historical/Getty Images, 38

Editor: Arnold Ringstad
Series Designer: Ryan Gale

Library of Congress Control Number: 2021941212

Publisher's Cataloging-in-Publication Data

Names: Gagne, Tammy, author.
Title: Smallpox / by Tammy Gagne
Description: Minneapolis, Minnesota : Abdo Publishing, 2022 | Series: Deadly diseases | Includes online resources and index.
Identifiers: ISBN 9781532196621 (lib. bdg.) | ISBN 9781098218430 (ebook)
Subjects: LCSH: Smallpox--Juvenile literature. | Smallpox--History--Juvenile literature. | Infectious diseases--Juvenile literature. | Epidemics--History--Juvenile literature. | Communicable diseases--Epidemiology--Juvenile literature.
Classification: DDC 614.49--dc23

CONTENTS

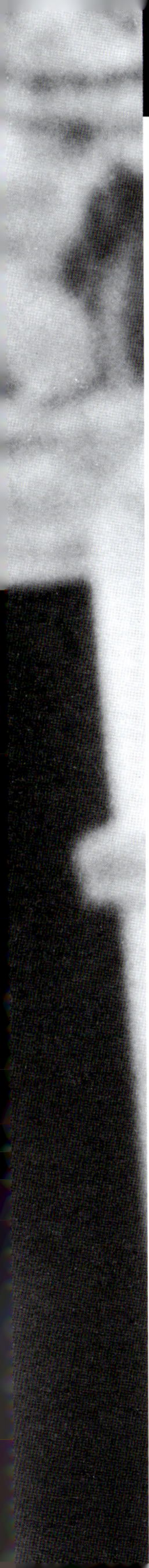

CHAPTER ONE

THE LAST CASE OF SMALLPOX

In October 1977, Ali Maow Maalin worked to save two children in Somalia. Both young girls had symptoms of a rare but dangerous illness called smallpox. Maalin had never had smallpox. He also hadn't had the vaccine for it. He knew he could catch the disease. He could even die from it. But the children needed medical attention quickly. He drove them to the nearest hospital.

A few days later, Maalin began feeling ill himself. His head ached. He also developed

Ali Maow Maalin caught the world's last case of smallpox through community spread.

PERSPECTIVES

EDUCATING PEOPLE ABOUT VACCINES

Sometimes good things arise from challenges. This was the case for Ali Maow Maalin after his battle with smallpox. Before, Maalin had been afraid of being vaccinated. Surviving the disease inspired him to teach others about the importance of vaccines. Maalin spent the rest of his life working as a vaccinator against another deadly illness, polio. He did not want Somalia to be the last nation in ending polio as it had been with smallpox. He said, "I tell [people] how important these vaccines are. I tell them not to do something foolish like me." In 2013 Maalin passed away from another dangerous disease called malaria.

a fever. Soon a rash appeared on his face and body. These raised bumps were symptoms of smallpox. The name of this disease comes from the Latin word for "spotted."

Shortly after Maalin's symptoms began, one of the girls he took to the hospital died. Maalin knew his own life was also at risk. Smallpox had killed more than 300 million people since the beginning of

A major vaccination campaign eliminated smallpox in Africa and around the globe.

the 1900s. It was no longer as common as it once had been. Nearly every country in the world had eradicated smallpox by 1976. But it was still spreading in Ethiopia, Kenya, and Somalia.

Maalin was lucky. He survived his battle with smallpox. He went down in history as the last case of smallpox from person-to-person transmission. On May 8, 1980, the World Health Organization (WHO) officially declared the illness eradicated. Smallpox is the only human infectious disease that has been eradicated worldwide.

WHAT IS SMALLPOX?

The variola virus causes smallpox. Viruses are microscopic objects that can infect humans. Once a virus enters the body, it invades living cells. It uses those cells to make copies of itself. Those copies then make more copies and so on. This process is how viruses make people sick. One of the most common viruses is influenza. It causes the flu. Most people who catch it fully recover in about one week.

The risk of dying from smallpox was much greater. About 30 percent of people who caught this illness died from it. Those who survived were often left with severe scars on their faces or bodies. Some survivors also lost their eyesight.

Smallpox began spreading more than 3,000 years ago. For centuries people did not know what caused the illness. They also didn't know how to prevent it from spreading. When a person developed the disease, family members and

FROM PERSON TO PERSON

Many diseases infect both humans and animals. Some can spread between species. But smallpox could be spread only from one human to another. This made it easier for scientists to stop it. If animals also carried the disease, stopping it would have been a much harder task.

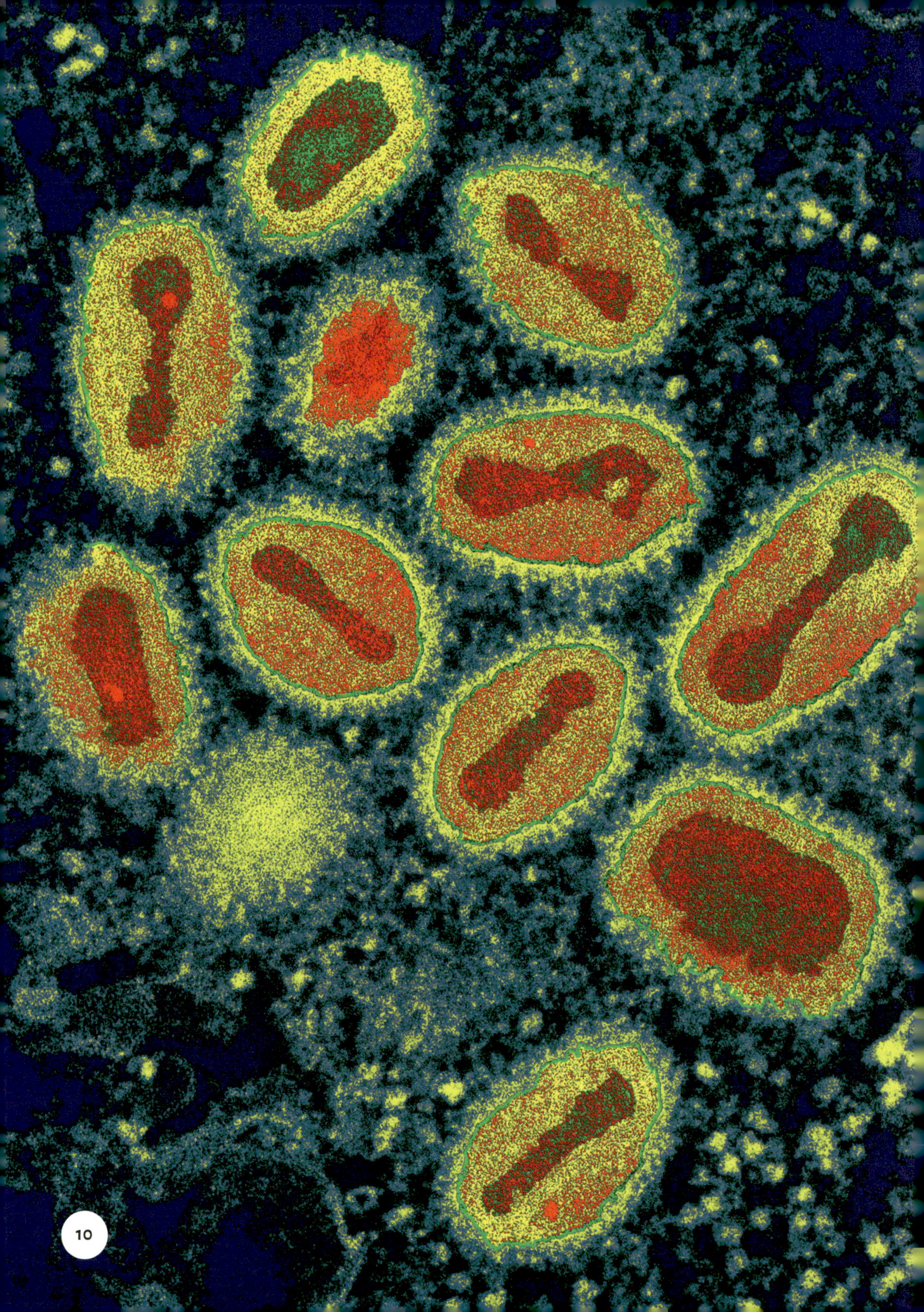

other caregivers tried to help. Many of them caught smallpox too.

For a long time it seemed nothing could be done to stop smallpox. Many people felt they could not avoid catching it. If they were especially fortunate, they would survive the disease. Eventually doctors learned the best way to stop smallpox from killing people. They had to prevent people from catching it in the first place.

FURTHER EVIDENCE

Chapter One discusses the smallpox virus. What is one of this chapter's main points? What evidence is included to support this point? Read the article at the website below. Does the information on the website support this point? Does it present new evidence?

SMALLPOX

abdocorelibrary.com/smallpox

The tiny smallpox virus was invisible to people until they invented the powerful microscopes needed to see it.

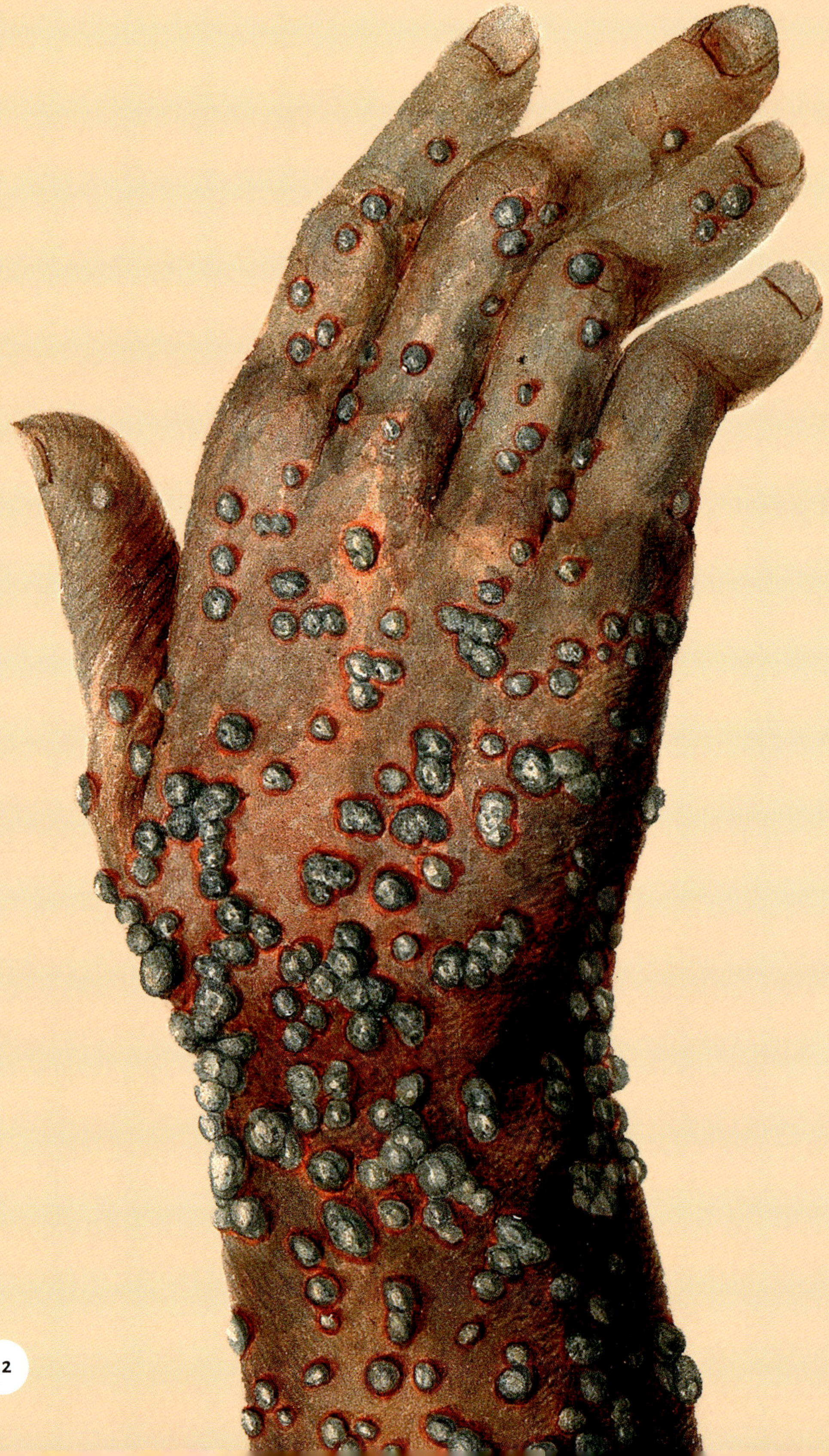

CHAPTER TWO

THE HISTORY OF SMALLPOX

Smallpox began thousands of years ago. No one knows exactly when. The first recorded case was in China in 340 CE. But many historians and scientists think the disease existed long before then in both Egypt and India. King Ramses V ruled Egypt between 1150 and 1145 BCE. Archaeologists found his mummy in 1898 CE. When they did, they saw that he had a rash on his face. The raised bumps looked a lot like the smallpox rash.

Smallpox was a part of life for humanity for thousands of years.

SMALLPOX AS A WEAPON

Smallpox was common in Europe, but it was new to North America. People's immune systems had few defenses against it. Most European settlers had no idea that they were carrying smallpox to the New World. But a few of them infected American Indians on purpose. British military leaders met with representatives of the Delaware people at Fort Pitt during the French and Indian War (1754–1763). Before the Delaware representatives left the meeting, they asked for supplies for their trip home. The British agreed. But they also gave the travelers two blankets and a handkerchief from a smallpox ward.

Smallpox began spreading around the globe in the 1400s CE. During this time, explorers traveled across oceans on ships. As people settled in new lands, trade between continents also spread smallpox. Trade routes expanded, and the disease reached more places.

Smallpox epidemics ravaged many areas. The disease was especially common in Europe in the 1700s and 1800s. As much as 60 percent

SMALLPOX ORIGINS

Smallpox was documented in China in 340 CE. But the disease may have been in Egypt or India even earlier. How might smallpox have traveled from these places to China in ancient times?

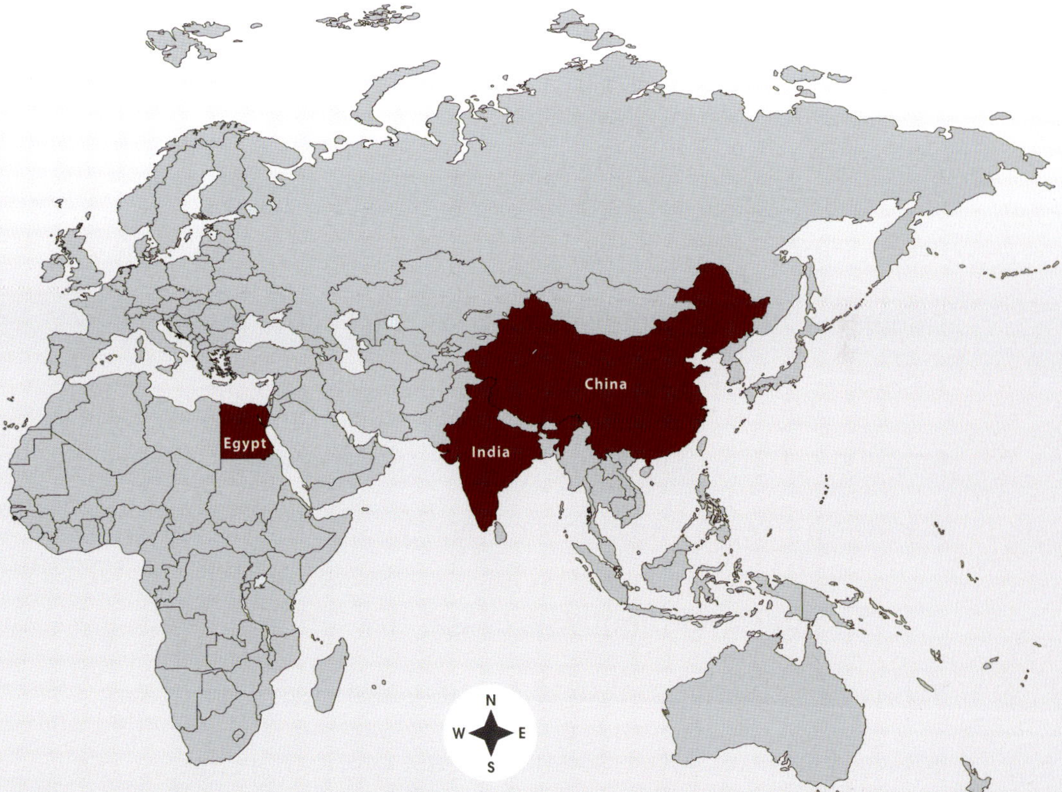

of the adults who caught it died. The death rate was even higher in infants. Nearly 80 percent of babies in London, England, who caught the illness did not survive.

EARLY AND UNUSUAL TREATMENTS

For centuries doctors did their best to treat people who had smallpox. Some of the earliest methods may seem bizarre compared with modern medicine. One of these treatments was called bloodletting. People believed that diseases were caused by having bad blood. They also thought that fevers were caused by having too much blood in the body. For these reasons many early healers would cut smallpox patients to allow them to bleed. But this approach did not help people with smallpox. Other doctors tried herbal remedies. These also didn't keep people from dying.

Another treatment was called the red treatment. It involved exposing patients to the color red. Caregivers would place red objects such as art or cloth in the

A Japanese illustration shows a warrior battling a god representing smallpox.

PERSPECTIVES

FEARING THE WORST

Fear of smallpox ran high wherever the virus struck. Outbreaks of the disease were especially common during the American Revolution (1775–1783). Most British soldiers had already fought and survived the disease back in England. But most Continental soldiers had no immunity to smallpox. They went to great lengths to avoid exposure. Connecticut governor Jonathan Trumbull once wrote, "The smallpox in our Northern army carries with it greater dread than our enemies. Our men dare face them but are not willing to go into a hospital."

rooms of smallpox patients. This technique began in Japan around 10 CE. Some doctors still used it in the United States and Europe in the 1900s. But the red treatment did not actually help people with smallpox.

People caring for smallpox patients eventually realized they had no effective treatment or cure. The most they could offer was supportive care. But even something as simple as providing a comfortable bed and fluids was challenging. Smallpox

For most of history, there was little doctors could do to effectively treat smallpox patients.

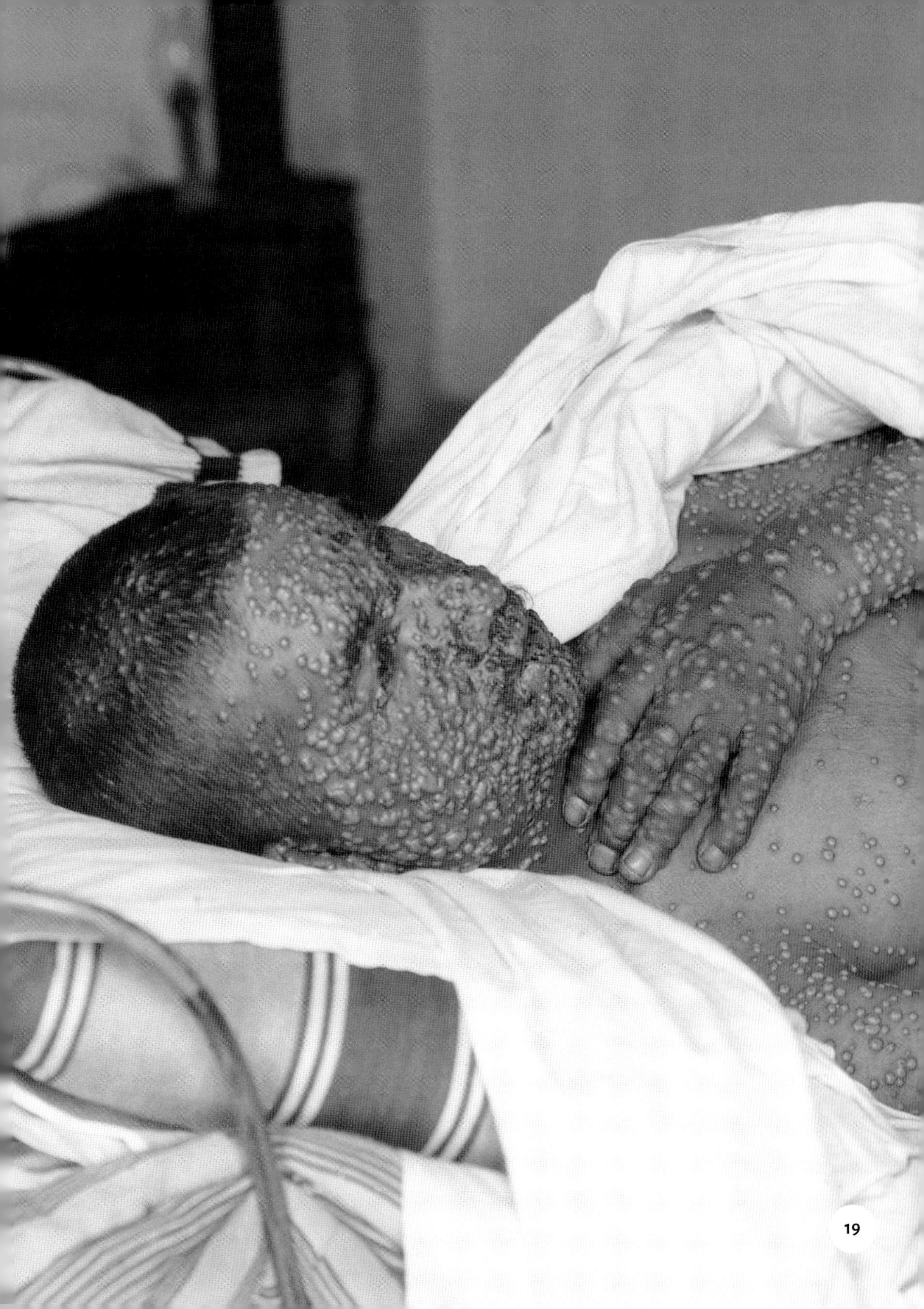

patients needed to be kept away from anyone who had not already had the disease. Otherwise they risked passing it on to others.

STOPPING THE SPREAD

In the early 1700s, many doctors focused on stopping smallpox from spreading. Some people who survived smallpox also got involved in these efforts. One of them was an English writer named Lady Mary Wortley Montagu. Although she survived smallpox as a young woman, the illness left her severely scarred. Upon traveling to Turkey with her husband, Montagu learned about variolation.

Variolation was a process that exposed people to the smallpox virus in a limited way. Doctors collected material from smallpox sores. Then they scratched it into the arms of people who had never had the illness. Some people inhaled the material through their noses instead. Most people who underwent variolation developed a fever and a rash. But they became less

Lady Mary Wortley Montagu was an early advocate for variolation in Europe.

likely to die of smallpox. When she returned to England, Montagu encouraged others to try variolation. But many doctors opposed this process. They did not think it was safe.

By the late 1700s, an English doctor named Edward Jenner had an idea that could protect people from

Jenner tested his smallpox vaccine on a young boy.

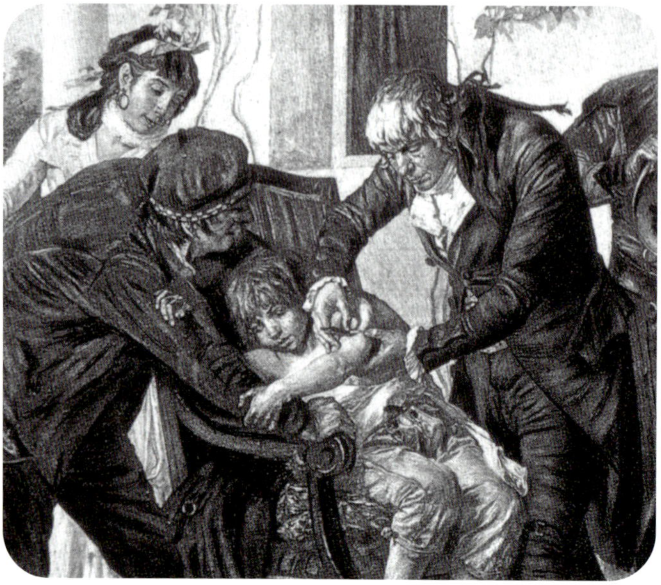

getting smallpox. A disease called cowpox was also spreading through England at this time. It was named for the animals that spread the illness to humans. Like smallpox, cowpox caused a sore to develop on the patient's skin. But cowpox was rarely fatal. Jenner noticed that milkmaids who'd had cowpox did not catch smallpox. He decided to try exposing people to cowpox to give them immunity against smallpox. It worked. Jenner's studies led him to create the vaccine for smallpox in 1796. It was the first successful vaccine ever developed.

STRAIGHT TO THE SOURCE

Dr. Donald R. Hopkins wrote an article about smallpox's impact on history in the *American Journal of Public Health*. In the piece, he wrote:

> *In the 80 years between 1694 and 1774, smallpox killed a queen of England, an Austrian emperor, a king of Spain, a tsar of Russia, a queen of Sweden, and a king of France. An example of the direct consequence of one such intervention was Emperor K'ang Hsi. He became one of the three greatest and longest reigning emperors of China, after having been raised to the Dragon Throne expressly because he alone among his father's three oldest sons had already had smallpox when his father, the first Manchu emperor, died of the disease in 1661.*

Source: Donald R. Hopkins. "Smallpox: Ten Years Gone." *American Journal of Public Health*, vol. 78, no. 12, 1988, p. 1590.

BACK IT UP

The author of this passage is using evidence to support a point. Write a paragraph describing the point the author is making. Then write down two or three pieces of evidence the author uses to make the point.

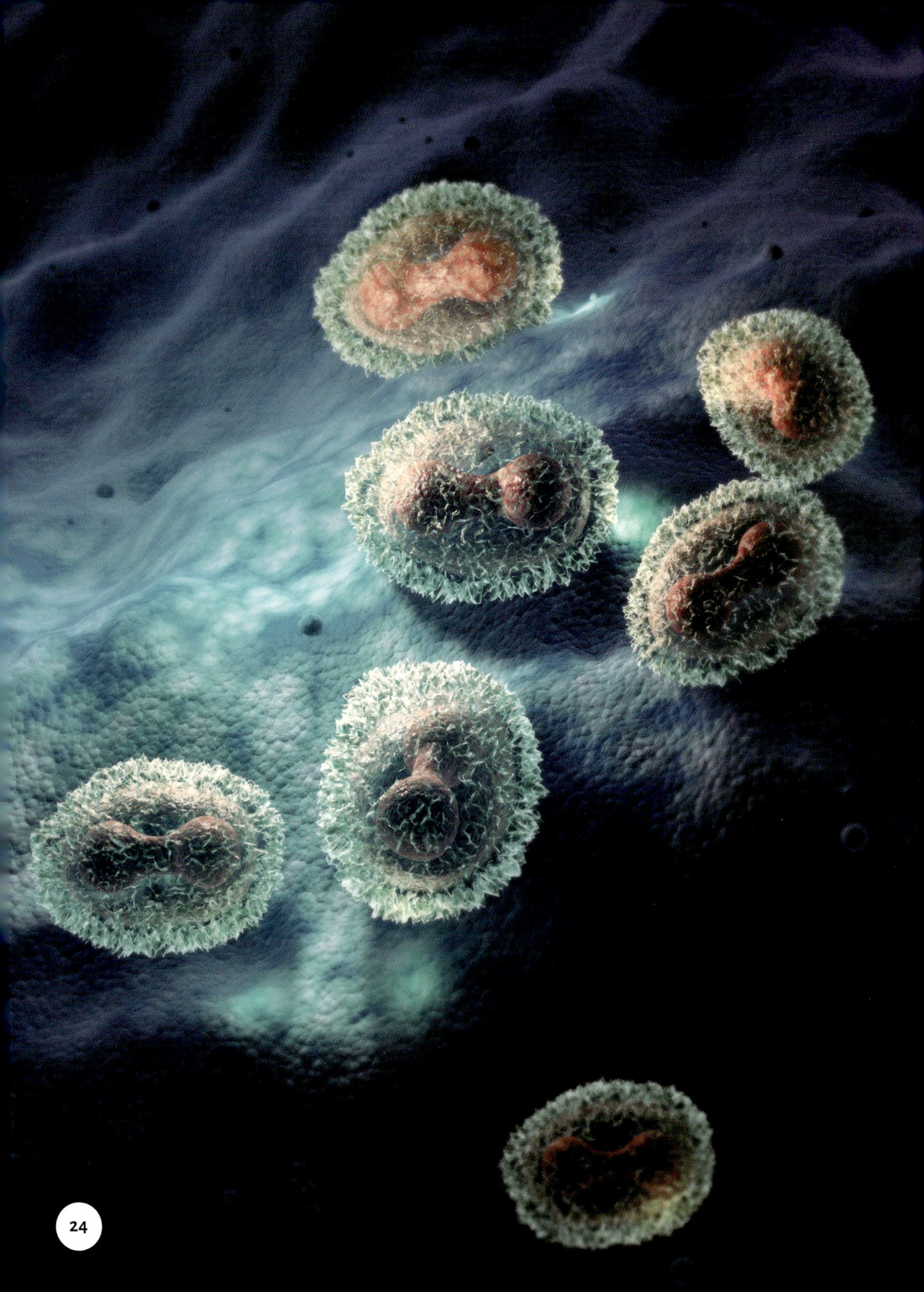

CHAPTER THREE

THE SCIENCE OF SMALLPOX

Viruses are tiny but powerful objects that exist everywhere on Earth. They cannot be seen without a microscope. But once they invade a living host, they can cause severe illness. They depend on the cells of their hosts. After a virus enters a body, it attaches to a cell. Then it uses that cell to make copies of itself. Some viruses cause only minor symptoms. For example, the common cold is caused by a virus. Other viruses can be deadly. Smallpox is in this category.

The smallpox virus is much smaller than the cells it attacks.

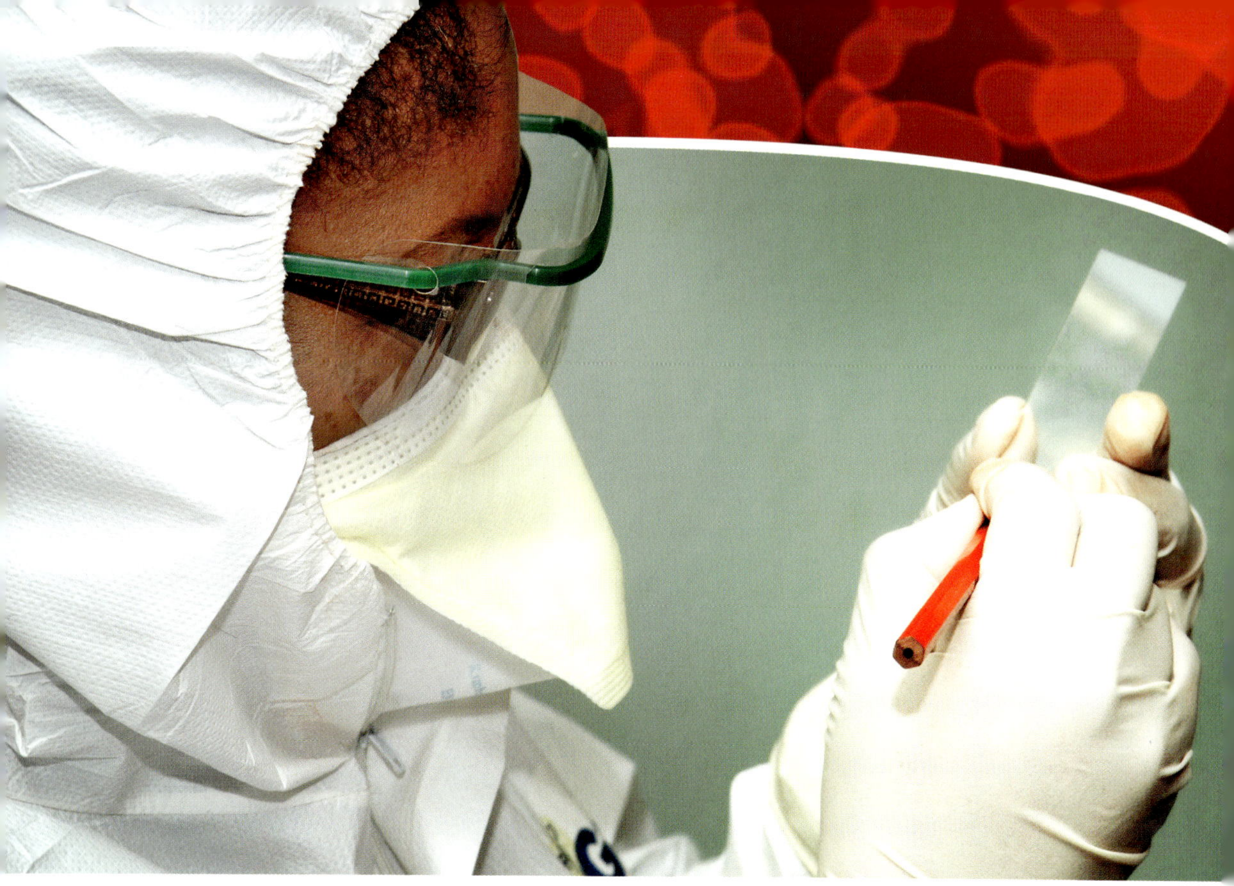

Special care must be taken when dealing with samples of the smallpox virus.

Viruses spread in a variety of ways. Some linger in the air. Others require direct contact with an infected person. Many people caught smallpox when an infected person coughed or sneezed near them. Items that smallpox patients touched, such as clothing or bedding, also passed the illness to others.

Smallpox patients had to be treated carefully for this reason. Doctors and nurses who worked with smallpox patients had to wear masks and gloves. Any items that came into contact with patients had to be thoroughly disinfected or thrown away. Laundry workers also had to wear gloves to lessen their risk of catching the disease.

THE ORIGINS OF SMALLPOX

No one knows for sure where smallpox came from. Some scientists think it might have evolved from a rodent poxvirus more than 10,000 years ago. But it did not start spreading widely until people began living in large cities. This allowed the virus to circulate through communities.

THE SYMPTOMS OF SMALLPOX

After people were exposed to smallpox, they could develop the illness between 7 and 19 days later. This is called the incubation period of an illness.

Most smallpox patients started showing symptoms in 10 to 14 days. The disease could not be passed to others during the incubation period. Most people also did not feel sick at this point.

Patients then developed a variety of symptoms. These included a fever as high as 105 degrees Fahrenheit (40.6°C), chills, and a general feeling of discomfort. A sore throat, headache, and backache were also common symptoms. Many patients also experienced severe abdominal pain and vomiting. This phase of the illness typically lasted about four days.

As the fever ended, the rash emerged. The first bumps usually erupted in the patient's throat and mouth. This was when a smallpox patient became contagious. Bumps then appeared on the face, limbs, and other areas of the body. After about a week, the raised bumps turned into pustules. The bumps remained in this state before forming into crusty scabs around a week later. The scabs began falling off a few days after that. Patients remained contagious until the last scab fell off. About 30 percent of the people who were infected with smallpox died.

LIFE AFTER SMALLPOX

Smallpox took a huge toll on the world in many ways. Some ancient cultures put off naming their children until smallpox struck the fragile newborns. The disease was so common that many parents just assumed that their newborns would catch it. Children faced even higher death rates from smallpox than adults. The few babies who survived smallpox were then given names.

PERSPECTIVES

IF SMALLPOX WERE TO RETURN

A smallpox outbreak today could devastate the world. Modern medicine has greatly increased the human life span. Elderly people, who often have weakened immune systems, would face high risks from smallpox. Medicine has also made it possible to live with many chronic diseases. But such diseases also weaken patients' immune systems. In 2018 disease researcher Raina MacIntyre led a study about how smallpox could affect today's largest cities. The study found that one in five people in cities such as New York and Sydney has a weakened immune system. These people would be less likely to survive smallpox.

Survivors of smallpox were often left with scars on their skin.

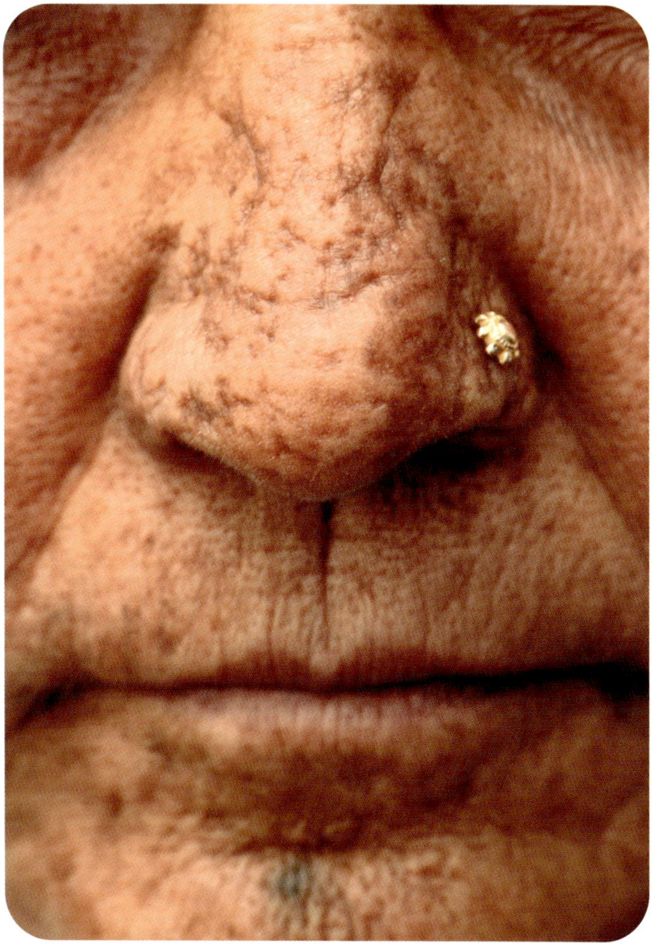

Many people who survived smallpox felt lucky to be alive. But they also faced new hardships. Between 65 and 80 percent of survivors had pockmarks on their skin for the rest of their lives. Often these scars were left on the victims' faces. This made life especially challenging for many of them.

An Indian man named Sundaram Parthasarathi beat smallpox when he was just six months old. But when he got older, some children called him mean names because of the marks on his face. In his sixties, he remembered not wanting to go to school because of the bullying. People who didn't make fun of him often stared. He also hated feeling as if people felt sorry for him.

EXPLORE ONLINE

The focus of Chapter Three is on the science of smallpox. The website below discusses the same topic. As you know, every source is different. How is the information at the website different from the information in this chapter? What information is the same? What information did you learn from the website?

KIDSHEALTH: SMALLPOX

abdocorelibrary.com/smallpox

CHAPTER FOUR

STOPPING SMALLPOX

By the 1800s, there was still no treatment or cure for smallpox. Health officials focused on keeping the disease from spreading. Doctors began placing people with smallpox in isolation. Patients were kept away from the public until they were no longer contagious. People with smallpox who were not sick enough to be in a hospital were also asked to isolate themselves.

Many people greatly feared smallpox because it was so deadly. This fear led to some

Vaccines were effective at stopping smallpox, but it took time for the public to build up trust in them.

extreme precautions. In 1901 the city of Cleveland, Ohio, sent disinfectant crews from house to house to spray formaldehyde. This chemical with a strong odor kills germs. But it is also dangerous if inhaled. For a while precautions like this seemed to stop the disease. But more outbreaks later took place.

Entire hospitals were built to care for smallpox patients. There still wasn't much doctors could do. They simply kept patients comfortable while the virus ran its course. But these facilities also served another important purpose. They kept patients with the illness away from the general public. Still, infection rates soared in urban areas through the early 1900s. In England, doctors noticed that infection rates in cities with smallpox hospitals were higher than in cities without them. But the rates were not higher near hospitals in more rural locations. For this reason, doctors recommended that smallpox hospitals be built far away from cities. They were desperate to keep infection rates down.

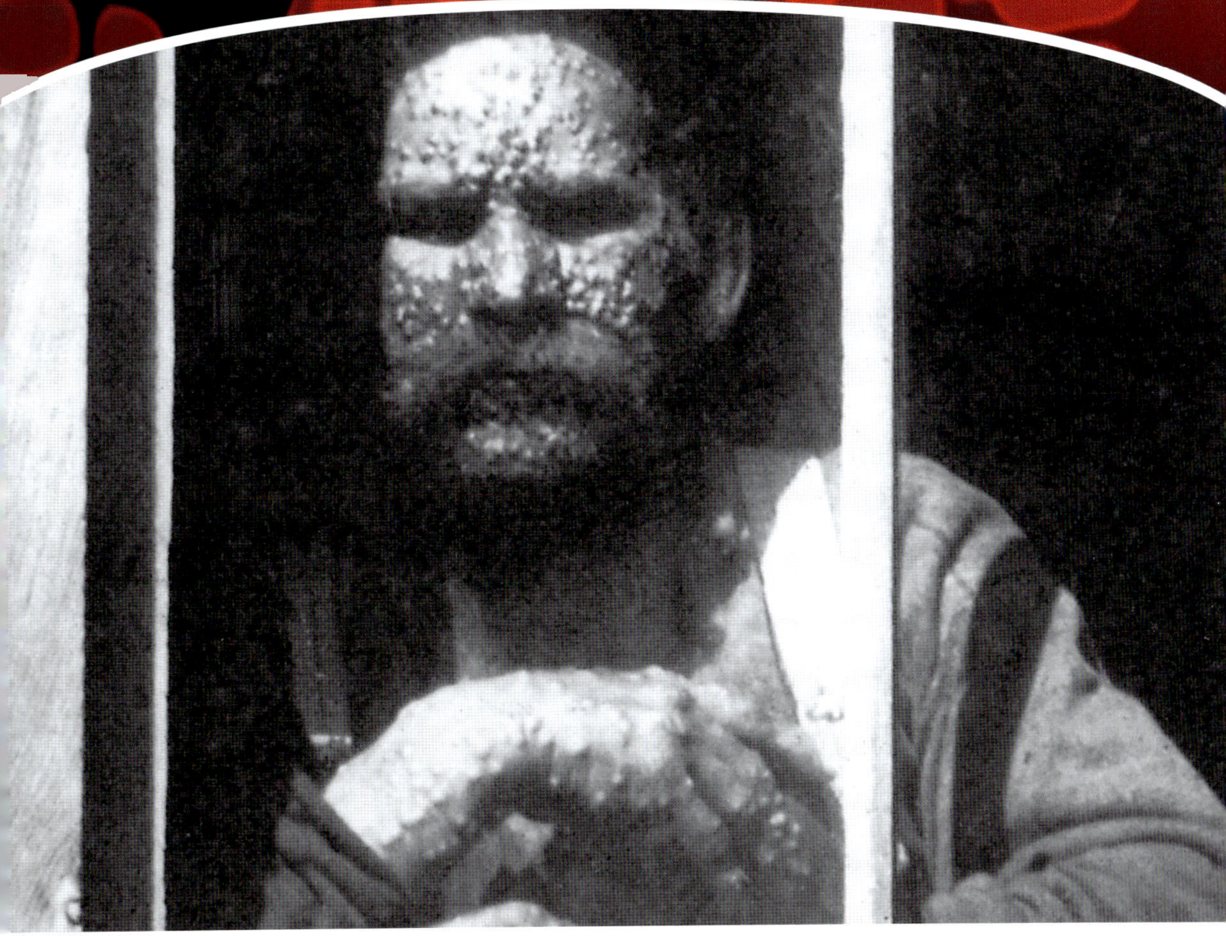

Isolation was once the only tool doctors had to slow the spread of smallpox.

PROBLEMS WITH EARLY VACCINES

The smallpox vaccine of 1796 was largely effective. But at first many people feared it even more than the virus. They did not know what to expect from this treatment since it was still so new. The idea of injecting a person with a virus seemed illogical to many. Their fears were only worsened when some people got sick from the vaccine.

The limits of transportation in the 1800s and early 1900s were also a problem. The fastest ways to travel were by train or ship. Batches of vaccine had a shelf life of weeks to months. But getting the vaccine to those who needed it could take a long time. Vaccines that sat too long became worthless. At best they were ineffective. At worst they were dangerous. Time and research helped solve this problem. Scientists learned how to preserve vaccines for longer periods. As smallpox vaccines became safer, more people agreed to receive them.

VACCINATING THE WORLD

The last case of smallpox in the United States was in 1949. But many other parts of the world continued to face the illness. A decade later, smallpox had been wiped out in North America, Europe, and Australia.

THE LAST 30 YEARS OF SMALLPOX

In the last 30 years before smallpox was eradicated, the annual reported worldwide cases dropped from more than 600,000 to zero. How does this graph help you better understand the discussion in the text regarding smallpox eradication?

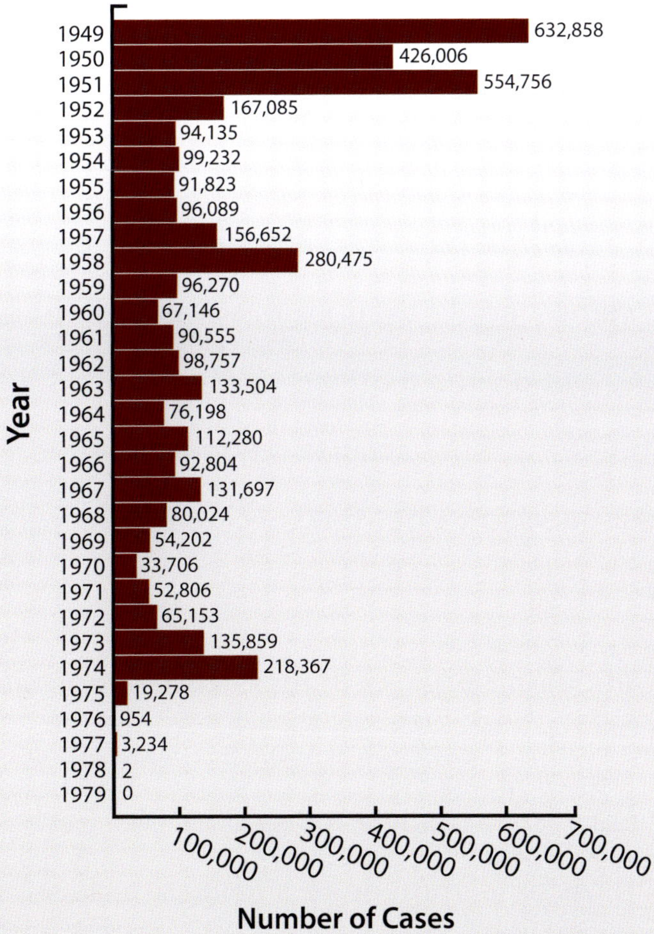

Kids in the United States receive smallpox vaccines in 1953.

It was still spreading in 60 countries in South America, Africa, and South Asia. In 1959 the World Health Organization (WHO) began a campaign to eradicate smallpox. Some people thought this was an impossible task. Wiping out a virus that had existed for so long would not be easy. But vaccines made it possible. Doctors just needed to get the vaccine to everyone who needed it.

The campaign began with mass vaccination sites all over the world. Health-care workers focused on getting shots into as many arms as possible. Each person who became immune to smallpox reduced the threat of future outbreaks. But the people who needed the vaccine most lived in areas where outbreaks were currently happening. At this point the strategy changed. Public health workers traveled to these regions to stop each outbreak. First, they quarantined the sick. Then they started vaccinating everyone who'd had contact with the sick people. This practice is known as ring vaccination.

The vaccination effort took an enormous amount of time and work. But it was successful. The last cases of smallpox

THE LAST SMALLPOX VICTIM

Medical photographer Janet Parker was the last person to die from smallpox. She was exposed in England while working at Birmingham's University Medical School in 1978. Experts think the virus was transported through ductwork in the building from a research lab. At that time, the world was very close to wiping out the illness. The most recent outbreak had been many years before. But Parker's case caused the medical community to worry about another outbreak happening.

were diagnosed in the late 1970s. And on May 8, 1980, the WHO declared smallpox eradicated from the world. Today the virus is no longer spreading. Most vaccinations for smallpox stopped in 1972 because the threat of the disease was gone. But doses of the vaccine are still kept in storage in case smallpox ever comes back.

PERSPECTIVES

DANGEROUS MATERIAL

Samples of the smallpox virus exist in two laboratories in the world. One is in the United States. The other is in Russia. These samples could be useful for producing new vaccines for the disease. Some people worry about the risk of an accident in the one of the labs or the virus being released on purpose. US health official Kathleen Sebelius explained why the samples must be kept. She wrote, "To do any less keeps future generations at risk from the re-emergence of one of the deadliest diseases humanity has ever known. Until this research is complete, we cannot afford to take that risk."

STRAIGHT TO THE SOURCE

Professor Arne Akbar is the president of the British Society for Immunology. On May 8, 2020, he issued a statement to the world as it faced another pandemic—COVID-19:

> *Today marks a big milestone in the history of immunology research—40 years since the eradication of smallpox, the only disease affecting humans ever to be completely eliminated. . . . The story of smallpox eradication reminds us all of the critical importance of vaccines and what we can achieve by working together as an international community against a public health threat. As the world deals with the current COVID-19 pandemic, our past success in eradicating smallpox should provide us with hope that, through scientific efforts and international cooperation, we can achieve a healthier and safer future for us all.*

Source: "40 Years since Smallpox Eradication." *BSI*, 8 May 2020, immunology.org. Accessed 21 June 2021.

WHAT'S THE BIG IDEA?

Take a close look at Akbar's words. What is his main idea? What evidence is used to support his point? Come up with a few sentences showing how Akbar uses evidence to support his main point.

IMPORTANT DATES

340 CE
The first recorded case of smallpox occurs in China.

1400s
Smallpox begins spreading around the world.

1796
Edward Jenner creates the first smallpox vaccine.

1949
The last smallpox case in the United States occurs.

1959
The World Health Organization (WHO) begins its campaign to eradicate smallpox worldwide.

1972
The United States stops vaccinating against smallpox.

1976
Smallpox is eradicated in every country except Ethiopia, Kenya, and Somalia.

1978
Smallpox claims the life of its last victim, Janet Parker.

1980
On May 8, the WHO declares smallpox eradicated from the world.

STOP AND THINK

Surprise Me

This book discusses smallpox, one of history's deadliest diseases. After reading this book, what two or three facts about smallpox did you find most surprising? Write a few sentences about each fact. Why did you find each fact surprising?

Dig Deeper

After reading this book, what questions do you still have about smallpox? With an adult's help, find a few reliable sources that can help you answer your questions. Write a paragraph about what you learned.

Take a Stand

Samples of the smallpox virus still exist in two labs. Some people think they should be saved in case the virus ever reemerges. Others think these samples could be used as weapons and should be destroyed. Write a short paragraph explaining your opinion.

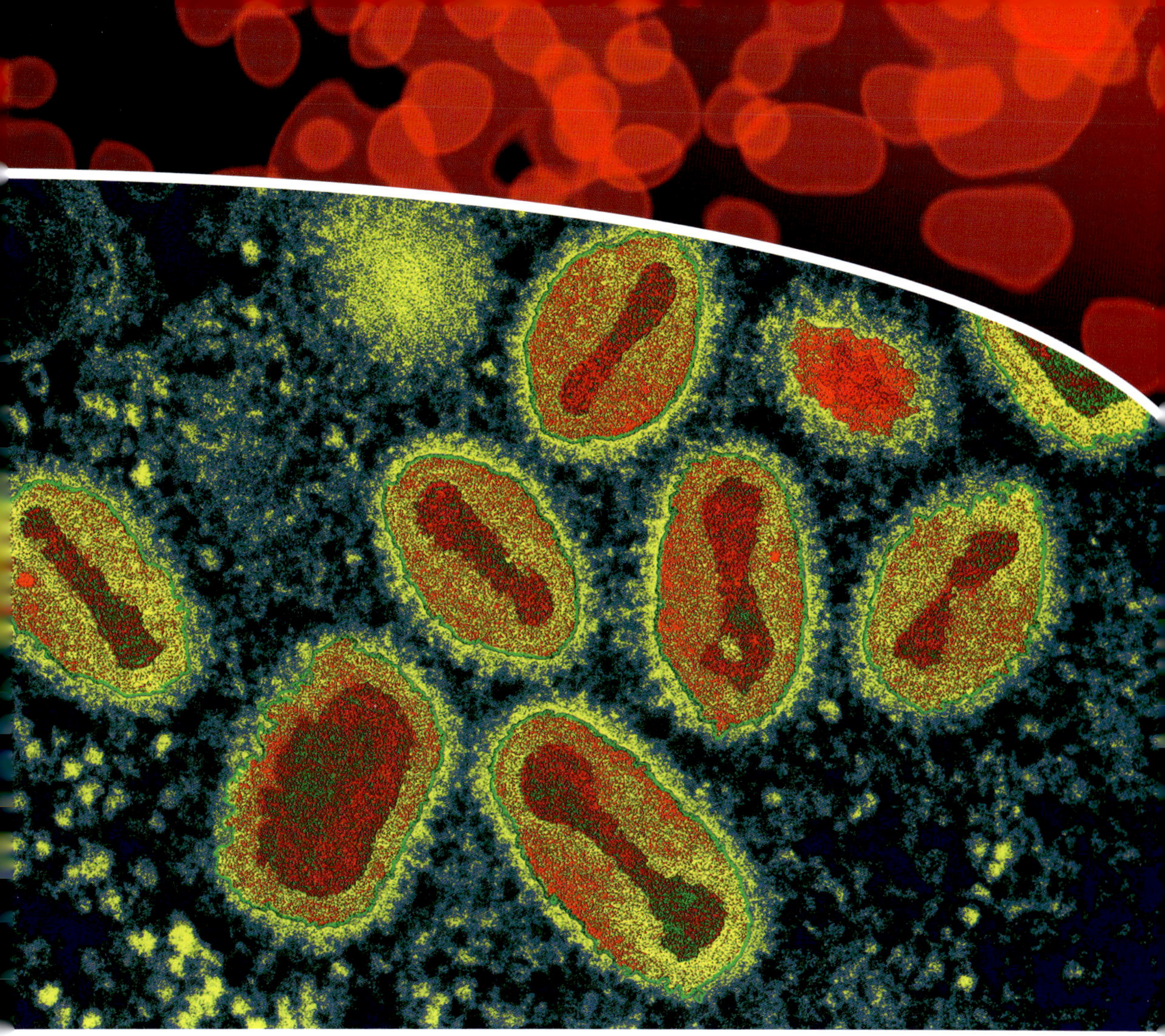

You Are There

Chapter Four talks about workers in Cleveland in the early 1900s disinfecting private homes with formaldehyde to stop smallpox from spreading. Imagine that you lived in Cleveland at this time. How would you feel about this decision? Write a paragraph to describe your opinions about it.

GLOSSARY

archaeologist
a person who studies history through artifacts and human remains

campaign
an organized course of action to achieve a goal

epidemic
a widespread occurrence of an infectious disease

eradicate
to completely eliminate an illness

immune system
the specialized cells, tissues, and organs of the body that prevent and fight infection

immunity
the ability to resist an infection from a disease

intervention
the process of interrupting a course of events

pustule
a blister on the skin containing a substance called pus

quarantine
a period of isolation to prevent the spread of disease

ONLINE RESOURCES

To learn more about smallpox, visit our free resource websites below.

Core Library CONNECTION
FREE! COMMON CORE MULTIMEDIA RESOURCES

Visit **abdocorelibrary.com** or scan this QR code for free Common Core resources for teachers and students, including vetted activities, multimedia, and booklinks, for deeper subject comprehension.

Booklinks NONFICTION NETWORK
FREE! ONLINE NONFICTION RESOURCES

Visit **abdobooklinks.com** or scan this QR code for free additional online weblinks for further learning. These links are routinely monitored and updated to provide the most current information available.

LEARN MORE

Cummings, Judy Dodge. *Epidemics and Pandemics: Real Tales of Deadly Diseases*. Nomad Press, 2018.

Hodgkins, Fran. *Finding a COVID-19 Vaccine*. ReferencePoint, 2021.

INDEX

About the Author

Tammy Gagne has written hundreds of books for both adults and children. Some of her recent books have been about media literacy and mental health. She lives in northern New England with her husband, her son, and several pets.